For.........................

Anke Kuhl

PERFECT PRESENTS!

Translated by Melody Shaw

GECKO PRESS

First American edition published 2023 by Gecko Press USA,
an imprint of Gecko Press Ltd.

This edition first published in 2022 by Gecko Press
PO Box 9335, Wellington 6141, Aotearoa New Zealand
office@geckopress.com

English-language edition © Gecko Press Ltd 2022
Translation © Melody Shaw 2022
© 2020 Anke Kuhl
© Kibitz Verlag for the original German edition
Translation made in arrangement with Am-Book Inc. (www.am-book.com)

Gecko Press is committed to sustainable practice. We publish books to be read over and over.
We use sewn bindings and high-quality production and print all our new books using vegetable
inks on FSC-certified paper from sustainably managed forests.

Original language: German
Typesetting by Katrina Duncan
Printed in China by Everbest Printing Co. Ltd,
an accredited ISO 14001 & FSC-certified printer

ISBN hardback: 9781776574995

For more curiously good books, visit geckopress.com